Unfinished Journey

未尽的旅程

by Snow Ray

Published by Majestic River Publisher, LLC
Hooksett, USA

CONTENTS

Unfinished Journey · (未尽的旅程)

Snow Ray

Introduction

In remembering Wen Wen's life, we are reminded not only of her kindness, her strength, but also of the silences and suffering that surrounded her. Too often, pain hides behind quiet smiles, and families—however loving—may fail to recognize how deep the wounds run felling helpless when unable to give the support so desperately needed. Wen Wen's parents, both educated and compassionate scholars, carried their regret like a lifelong shadow.

Their grief reminds us that understanding and love are essential, but without timely social and medical help, irreversible harm may still befall those we hold dear.

前言

在回望温文的一生时，我们不仅被她的善良与坚韧所打动，也被她生命中那份无声的痛楚所震撼。太多时候，痛苦隐藏在沉默与微笑之后；再深的爱，也未必能看清一个人心底的伤有多深。家人们在无力的关切中，常常感到无助与自责。

她的父母都是学者，通情达理，却一生背负着无法弥补的遗憾。他们的悲痛让我们明白：理解与爱固然重要，但若缺乏及时的社会与医学帮助，悲剧仍可能降临在我们最亲爱的人身上。

PROLOGUE

The Day I Returned

I had not set foot in our city for many years. Work carried me far away; life carried me further. People say distance softens pain. It does not. It only stores it.

I returned for one reason — my sister's grave.

Morning fog clung to the mountain as I walked through the old cemetery, laid out with quiet beauty. The names on the stones were familiar: my parents' colleagues, my grandparents, my grandfather's comrades who had fallen in war or faded in its aftermath. A few steps to the right of my parents, I found hers. A plain white stone, engraved with a name that still makes my heart pause: Wen Wen.

I placed roses there — ordinary, wordless, red as the last light of dusk.

For decades I told myself I left because leaving was the only way to survive. Yet I know everything

I became began with what she lost. When she was sent west, a space opened for me in a city factory. Later, I was chosen for a workers-and-peasants-student cohort. After reform, I studied abroad. I walked through doors forever closed to her. I crossed the corridors of libraries she once dreamed of.

I have mastered the language of reports, results and facts. But none of that language can contain my sister's life. So, I will write what I remember — not to explain, for history explains nothing — but to keep her from vanishing a second time.

This is her story.

CHAPTER 1

A House of Books

Her name was Wen Wen—written in Chinese as 温文, with Wen as her family name and Wen as her given name. Together, the characters meant gentleness and refinement. My parents had chosen the name in hope that their daughter, even in turbulent times, would carry herself with grace and learning.

My own name was Wen Ming, 温明, meaning "bright and enlightened." At home and among friends I was called Mingzi, a nickname that carried the warmth of childhood. Placed together, our names formed the word "civilization" (文明) — a reflection of our parents' belief that through us, culture and knowledge would endure.

Our childhood home was filled with books. The shelves sagged under their weight—histories, novels, and volumes of poetry that my father recited with ease. He was not only a professor but also a dean at the university, a man whose learning carried dignity yet never arrogance. My mother, a researcher of rare insight, balanced scholarship with quiet warmth. Between them, our home became a refuge of words and ideas, a place where even in uncertain times we felt the weight of culture like an anchor.

Evenings were our favorite hours. Father would sit beneath the lamp and read aloud—lines from ancient poems, passages from history, stories that stretched beyond the walls of our home. Wen Wen listened with rapt attention, her eyes luminous in the glow, while I leaned against her shoulder, too young to grasp every meaning but carried along by the cadence of his voice. Mother would sometimes add her own reflections, soft and precise, like brushstrokes on a canvas already vivid.

Wen Wen was the pride of our family. Two years older than me, she carried herself with an elegance beyond her age. Teachers praised not only her diligence but her kindness, the way she quietly helped classmates without expecting recognition. At home, she was my anchor—patient, encouraging, never too busy to share a story she had read or to guide my faltering hand across the page.

I was mischievous, quick to abandon study for play, but she never scolded harshly. Instead, Wen Wen drew me back with her calm example, her belief that books could open doors even when the world outside seemed intent on closing them. Her gentleness was not weakness but a quiet strength, and though I did not understand it then, I would carry its memory all my life.

Those early years were wrapped in a fragile peace. The walls of our home seemed to keep chaos at bay, though whispers of unrest drifted in from beyond—the rising storms of politics, the weight of history pressing closer. My parents, perhaps, knew that the tide would one day reach us. Yet in those moments, beneath the glow of lamplight and the rustle of turning pages, it felt as if we lived in a world apart: a home of books, of dreams, and of hope.

CHAPTER 2

Shadows Gathering

The world outside our home was changing, though at first it reached us only in whispers. At school, teachers grew cautious, their words trimmed of meaning. Neighbors spoke in lowered voices, glancing around before daring to mention politics. The air itself seemed to hold a tension, as if the city were bracing for a storm no one could name.

I was still a boy, restless and easily distracted, but even I could sense the unease. Posters appeared on walls—bold characters in red ink shouting slogans I barely understood. Crowds gathered in the streets, voices raised in chants that thrilled and frightened me at once. Wen Wen walked beside me, her hand steady on my arm, her face calm though her eyes betrayed thought. She was old enough to understand more than she said, careful never to speak carelessly, even to me.

At home, our parents carried on as if nothing had changed. Father still read and wrote in the evenings, his brush moving steadily across the page. Yet sometimes his gaze drifted toward the window, as though the silence beyond carried questions too heavy to voice—about the family's safety, about the university's uncertain future. Mother grew quieter, her research interrupted by sudden meetings and new demands from the institution. There was a heaviness in their movements, as though each day required more effort to preserve the fragile peace within our walls.

One evening, I found Wen Wen at her desk, copying lines from a book into her notebook. The lamplight fell across her face, serene and intent. I asked her why she bothered when the world seemed so uncertain. She smiled faintly, turning a page.

"Because words endure," she said. "They remind us who we are."

It was a simple answer, yet it struck me deeply. Even then, I knew my sister carried a strength greater than my own—a strength rooted not in

16

defiance but in quiet conviction. She seemed to understand that storms would come, that books might be taken, voices silenced, but the memory of truth could not be erased.

In the distance, the city rumbled with noise and fever. But within our home, for a little while longer, we clung to the rhythm of study and story, holding fast to the fragile threads of normal

CHAPTER 3

Storm Entered Our Home

The storm that had rumbled outside finally broke through our doors. What had once been whispers in the street and rumors in the marketplace arrived in our own home with banners, shouting, and fists.

Father was no longer a professor, no longer a dean. He was called a "reactionary academic," dragged to meetings where students and former colleagues denounced him with rehearsed fury. His books were seized, his desk overturned, his careful notes scattered like debris. At first, he tried to stand tall, to answer with reason, but soon even reason was forbidden. I saw his shoulders bend under the weight of insults, his silence becoming his only defense.

Mother fared no better. She had been a researcher of quiet brilliance, respected for her precision, her insight. But those qualities had no place in the fever of the times. She was paraded in the courtyard, her head forced down, a placard hung around her neck. I will never forget the look on her face—neither defiance nor despair, but a stunned disbelief, as if she could not comprehend that knowledge itself had become a crime.

Neighbors whispered warnings, urging our parents to burn their library before it brought greater danger. They had heard of professors in other cities whose homes had been raided, their treasured collections dragged into the street and set ablaze.

Father hesitated, his hands trembling as he touched the spines of books he had gathered over a lifetime—volumes of poetry, philosophy, histories, and his own writings. He could not bring himself to destroy them.

But choice was soon taken from him. One afternoon, Red Guard students stormed into our home. With shouts and jeers, they pulled the books from the shelves, armful after armful, and hurled them into the courtyard. Before our parents' eyes, the flames leapt high, consuming their life's work, the very pages that had once filled our nights with meaning. The air thickened with acrid smoke, heavy with the scent of paper and ink—bitter as if history itself were being erased before us.

In the chaos, Wen Wen acted with quiet resolve. She gathered a few small volumes—international classics in translation—and hid them deep beneath an old wooden box in a corner of the kitchen, a place no one would think to search. It was a fragile act of defiance, but in that moment, it felt like salvation.

That night, she sat beside me in silence. She did not weep, though her face was sad. At last she said, almost in a whisper,

"We must remember. Even if they take everything, we must remember."

Her words stayed with me. The storm had entered our home, tearing down the walls of safety we once believed unshakable. Yet in that ruin, my sister's quiet vow became a light I would carry always.

CHAPTER 4

A Secret Written in Verse

The final year of middle school should have been a time of promise. For Wen Wen, it was meant to open the doors to high school, to further study, to the life she had dreamed of since childhood. She was the best in her class—her essays read aloud as models, her calligraphy admired, her teachers certain she would have a bright future. But in those days, grades and talent counted for almost nothing.

When the list of students recommended for high school was posted, her name was missing. Not because she lacked ability, but because of our parents. Father had been branded a "reactionary academic," and Mother condemned as a "reactionary expert." Such labels alone were enough to erase her future.

That afternoon she returned home, books clutched against her chest. Father tried to comfort her, and Mother gently embraced her. Wen Wen said little, only a faint smile, as if to ease their guilt and worry. Yet later, I found her in her room, a notebook lying open, with a single line written in the margin: "The road has ended, but the heart keeps moving forward."

It was her secret verse, hidden where no one else would see.

Wen Wen was not alone in her loss. Her quiet classmate, Ji Chang, bore a heavy fate of his own. His father, once a respected university professor, was branded a Rightist during a political campaign. Stripped of his position, he was sent to labor in a factory, and the family lived under the shadow of disgrace. However beautiful Ji Chang's essays, however bright his eyes when he spoke of poetry, the gates of high school remained closed to him under the newly imposed admission system.

Perhaps that was why the two of them understood each other so deeply. In those final months, when classrooms echoed not with knowledge but with slogans, they began to exchange poems in secret. A folded scrap of paper slipped across a desk. A reply tucked into a book. Verses of rain and lamplight, of rivers and fog, of shadows and hope.

Their words never named "love"—they could not. In those times, even friendship among young people was closely watched, and romance was forbidden. Yet in those fragments of verse lay a tenderness that needed no confession. In a world that denied them both a future, poetry became their refuge, a way of speaking the unspeakable.

As graduation neared, classmates exchanged small tokens: a worn pen, a bookmark, a few torn pages from an old book. Wen Wen, however, had saved for weeks to buy something more. On the final day, she handed Ji Chang a brand-new notebook—its cover pale blue, its pages blank, waiting to be filled. On the first page she had written, in her neat hand: "Keep writing. One day, I believe you'll become a great poet."

Her hands trembled as she gave it to him. He accepted it as though it carried more than paper—as though it held her trust, her faith, and the fragile hope of a future they both feared was already lost.

He accepted the notebook, his eyes wide, as if the object weighed more than its paper and binding. For a moment he said nothing. Then, very softly: "Thank you."

The silence between them felt alive. Neither dared say more. Around them, the courtyard buzzed with students laughing too loudly, hiding their fear with noise.

That night Wen Wen lay awake, staring at the ceiling. She imagined him opening the notebook, imagined him writing poems that would carry his sadness and hope. She told herself she had done something small but real: she had given him a place to keep his words, to keep himself.

She did not know then that this would be her last gift—the final gesture before history's tide swept them apart.

CHAPTER 5

After the Parting

I still remember the silence after the school closed. It was not the silence of peace, but the kind that follows a verdict. My sister Wen Wen had been the brightest in her grade. If the world had been fair, she would have gone straight to the best high school in the city.

But in those years, fairness was a word with no meaning. Father had been branded a "reactionary academic authority." Mother was forced into endless labor reform. By those labels alone, Wen Wen was pushed into the shadows, counted among the children of the so-called "black categories." Her talent and excellence meant nothing.

For nearly a year after middle school, she stayed at home. Days blurred into repetition: cooking, cleaning, helping Mother when she returned exhausted, and watching over me. Sometimes she read by the dim lamp, her lips moving silently as if each line of poetry could hold the broken world together. Other times she stood at the window, gazing at the street where youths marched in groups, red armbands bright on their sleeves, shouting slogans that had nothing to do with us.

The Revolution grew wilder. Struggle sessions, parades, arrests—each day the city felt less like home. Father came and went with heavier steps, until one day he did not return at all.

A few months later, I too was told that I could no longer attend school. I never even graduated from middle school; I became an unemployed youth. In those days, only my sister remained at my side, caring for me and encouraging me to keep studying on my own.

For our safety, Mother made the hardest decision. She sent Wen Wen to our aunt's home in the south, while I was placed with other relatives nearby. We did not protest. Even as children, we understood that no one could argue with the storms of history.

That was how our paths began to separate—two young lives scattered by fear, while the world insisted it was for our "re-education."

Looking back, I realize it was in those quiet months at home that my sister first learned endurance. She carried her books like contraband, guarded her silence like a shield, and buried her sorrow deep inside. It was a lesson that would follow her all her life.

CHAPTER 6

A Gray Morning

I remember the morning my sister left for our aunt's home in the south. The sky was heavy with clouds, the air damp as though the city itself had grown weary of shouting. Wen Wen carried a small bag—just a change of clothes and a few books she refused to leave behind.

Mother's eyes were red but resolute. She pressed Wen Wen's hand and whispered, "Stay there until things become clearer. Your aunt and uncle will care for you. Don't worry about us."

Father was already gone—taken away, though no one told us where. Mother worked long hours; her body bent with exhaustion. There was no way she could keep both children safe under the same roof. So, she made the only choice she could: to scatter us, hoping distance might shield us from suspicion.

Wen Wen boarded the crowded train south. She leaned out of the window once before it pulled away. I still see her face in memory: troubled yet resigned, carrying a maturity beyond her years. There was strength in her beauty, a quite courage I did not yet understand.

When she arrived in Hangzhou, our aunt and uncle welcomed her warmly. In a way, she was fortunate—they had no children of their own, and quickly grew fond of her. To them, she was not the daughter of a "black category," but a bright, well-mannered girl. On weekends they took her to West Lake, walking together beneath the willows. Sometimes they told her stories of Mother's youth—how clever and beautiful she had been, how she once dreamed of becoming a professor herself.

But even in that gentler city, shadows lingered. Wen Wen knew she was living on borrowed time, sheltered only temporarily from the storm. Letters from Mother arrived slowly, each one beginning with a quotation from the Chairman Mao, and only afterward slipping in a line of tenderness: "Your brother is safe. I am fine. Study when you can. Mother misses you."

It was those lines, more than food or clothes, that sustained her. Looking back, I think that was the first time my sister learned how fragile happiness could be. The lake was beautiful, the willows graceful, but beneath it all lay silence: Father's absence, Mother's suffering, the weight of a family name no one dared to speak aloud.

CHAPTER 7

Meeting by the Lake

Hangzhou was nothing like our northern city. Wen Wen wrote that the air felt softer there, carrying the scent of willow branches and lake water. On weekends, our aunt and uncle often took her to West Lake, where small boats drifted gently, and young couples walked the shaded paths. In one of her letters, she told me it was the first time she had seen beauty not buried beneath dust and slogans.

It was there, by the lake, that she met Da Chuan. His mother worked with our aunt at the hospital. He was about her age—tall, with clear eyes and a quiet confidence. His parents had once been officials, but like so many others, they had fallen when the political tides turned. Yet he carried himself with a steadiness that seemed to say the world would one day open again.

What drew Wen Wen most was his music. He played the erhu with rare skill, its notes lingering over the park like threads of sorrow and strength woven together. Wen Wen had once led her school's performance troupe, singing and dancing before crowds. She understood the language of music, and with Da Chuan she felt an instant kinship. Music, she told me, was a language politics could not corrupt.

Their conversations began simply—about the lake, the weather, the shapes of clouds on the water. Gradually, they spoke of books, of half-remembered songs, and of futures no one dared to name. With Da Chuan, Wen Wen found she could speak more freely than she had in years. He listened intently, never mocking her seriousness.

For Da Chuan, Wen Wen was a mirror— intelligent, resilient, carrying a grace born of hardship but unbent by it. He admired her courage, though he never said so outright.

In those days, companionship itself was precious. Two young people walking side by side by the lake, sharing laughter and stories—that was enough to make them forget, for a little while, the posters on the walls and the rumors of arrests in the markets.

That moment by the lake was when Wen Wen allowed herself to hope again. It was not yet love, not entirely. But it was a beginning—a fragile, dangerous, profoundly human longing that would shape all that followed.

CHAPTER 8

Friendship

Life with our aunt and uncle soon settled into a quiet rhythm. Wen Wen helped with housework, read in the still afternoons, and sometimes accompanied our aunt to the market. Yet I know her heart lifted most when she walked by the lake with Da Chuan.

They never spoke of politics; there was no need. Instead, they shared the parts of themselves untouched by the storm. Wen Wen told him of her school days—how she once led classmates in songs and dances on stage. He spoke of learning music from his father's friends, of how the erhu had become his companion when words failed.

When Da Chuan played, Wen Wen sometimes sang along softly. Their voices blended—his strings steady, her voice clear and pure. It was a fragile harmony, yet it carried across the water like a promise that youth could still be beautiful, even in those years.

But shadows followed. Letters from home arrived irregularly, each one a mix of official slogans and hidden tenderness. Our mother, still under labor reform. Our father, absent and whispered about. And myself—I managed to write her only once, a letter full of strong words as if I could protect her from afar. She read it with tears; I later learned she knew I was more alone than I admitted.

Still, when walking beside Da Chuan, she tried to keep a brave expression. He, too, had known hardship—his father once punished, his mother often anxious. Yet he rarely spoke of it. Instead, he lightened the air with gentle jokes or urged her to tell stories. I believe he wanted to shield her from sorrow, to give her something lighter to hold.

Their friendship deepened quietly. To others, they were just two young people strolling by the willow-lined banks. But for Wen Wen, those walks became a sanctuary, a pause in a world that gave her no other refuge.

Their friendship gave her a place to breathe, a sense of being seen. For the first time in a long while, she carried not only burdens but also a fragile hope. It was the beginning of something that made her both happy and afraid.

CHAPTER 9

The Turning of Fate

In those months in Hangzhou, Wen Wen's life seemed quieter than it had been in years. She read from my uncle's bookcase, helped with household chores, and walked often by the lake. Beside Da Chuan, she sometimes felt as though the storm had loosened its grip, just a little.

But beyond the willow-lined banks, the world was shifting again. Rumors spread through the city: professors quietly restored to their posts, long-stalled institutions humming back to life, yet more young people sent away to the countryside and the frontier. Chaos had not ended—it had only changed its shape.

Da Chuan's family, too, was touched by the change. His father, once punished as a "mistaken" military officer, was partly reinstated, old connections stirred awake. And Da Chuan himself—gifted, steady, and with music that seemed to rise above the noise—began to attract notice.

One evening, he confided to Wen Wen in a low voice: he had been chosen for the army, not as a common soldier but as part of a performing troupe.

"They call us wenyibing (art soldier)," he explained, half proud, half apologetic. "We'll travel, play music, lift morale. It won't be easy, but…". He didn't finish. He didn't have to. For many families, a son in uniform was the highest honor, a badge of survival and pride. For Da Chuan, it was not just recognition—it was a door to a future.

Wen Wen forced a smile, though her heart must have ached. "You'll be remarkable," she told him softly. "They will love your music."

When Da Chuan left, the air by the lake felt different-emptier, quieter. It was their first parting, they would never meet again, except through the letters that carried their love across the years.

CHAPTER 10

Return to the Family

By then, Father was still imprisoned, Mother still bent beneath the weight of endless "reform through labor." Her letters arrived thin and cautious. Between the lines filled with political slogans, she always managed to slip in a few tender words: Take care of yourself. Don't worry about us.

Da Chuan had already gone, and Wen Wen was nearing sixteen. One morning, she turned to our aunt and said quietly, almost matter-of-factly: "I must go back to my mother. She's alone now."

Our aunt pleaded with her to stay. The city was not yet safe, Red Guards still prowled the streets. But Wen Wen's resolve was steady. She packed her cloth bag once again and boarded the northbound train.

When she stepped into our city, it was both familiar and foreign. The walls still shouted with slogans, shops were bare, neighbors still spoke in whispers. Yet to Wen Wen, even in its fear and scarcity, the city smelled of home.

I remember the moment she crossed our threshold. Mother, thinner than ever and streaked with white, lit up with a joy no hardship could suppress. She held Wen Wen so tightly it was as though she feared she might vanish again.

I had come too, taller now, more withdrawn. I no longer spoke much, but I had learned to shop for food, to tend the house, to answer the neighbors with silence when questions cut too close. Wen Wen saw the change in me—pride and sadness all at once.

Father's absence hung like a locked door above us, always there, never spoken of. At night, Wen Wen would lie awake, listening to Mother's weary breathing, wondering how much longer she could endure.

And yet, she did not regret returning. In a time when so much was being torn apart, simply being together was its own form of defiance. She cooked, she cleaned, she slipped open the few books that had survived the purges. She was not only a daughter, not only a sister—she became the thread that held what remained of our family together.

CHAPTER 11

The Westward Decision

That winter after Wen Wen's return was colder than most. Each day she rose early to help our mother—cooking, cleaning, fetching water—and even tried to sew clothes for us. She never complained, but in her eyes, I could catch the flicker of silent calculation, as if weighing the future only she could see.

Work was scarce. The factories favored the children of workers and cadres. For us, the schools remained barred. Father was still gone, Mother still bent to endless shifts of labor, her withheld wages barely enough to keep us afloat.

One evening, over a simple meal, Wen Wen set down her chopsticks and looked at Mother.

"If I go to the frontier," she said softly, "I can earn wages. I can support myself—and maybe even help you. And if I leave, perhaps my brother will have a better chance to stay here and find work."

Mother froze, chopsticks suspended in midair. For a long moment she said nothing, only stared at her daughter's face. At last, she sighed.

"You're still so young…"

"I'm not too young," Wen Wen replied. Her voice was steady. "Others are going. Why not me?"

In the corner, I sat listening, my heart hammering. I wanted to protest, to beg her not to go. But I knew her choice was not for herself—it was for us, for Mother, for the empty place where Father should have been.

Outside, the loudspeakers blared the same slogans day after day: Knowledgeable youth, go to the countryside! To the frontier! To where the motherland needs you most! Some shouted with conviction, others whispered their dread in the dark. Wen Wen listened but showed no fear. Perhaps she believed sacrifice could still mean hope; or perhaps she simply saw no other path.

At last, Mother's eyes filled with both pride and sorrow. "If you must go," she whispered, "promise me one thing: write often. Let me know you are safe."

Wen Wen nodded. She did not cry. Silence was her armor.

Looking back, I see how decisive that night was. She might have stayed longer beneath Mother's wing. Instead, she chose the unknown, shouldering a burden far heavier than her years.

And so, as the new year began, her road turned westward—toward Tibet, toward a life where hardship and hope would walk side by side.

CHAPTER 12

Departure

The morning she left was bitter cold, the sky low and gray. At the station, the platform swarmed with young people carrying canvas rucksacks bound with rope. Mothers clung to their children's hands until the last possible moment; fathers barked hurried instructions; friends exchanged promises they could never be sure to keep.

Wen Wen stood among them, slight in her dark coat, her bundle of clothes and a small packet of biscuits clasped tight. And, of course, her notebook—always her notebook. I remember her face that day: flushed by the cold wind, radiant with youth and quiet resolve, her eyes bright with courage to face an unknown world.

Mother tried to sound firm, but her lips trembled. "Take care of yourself. Write often. If you face hardship, tell me."

Wen Wen only nodded. I knew she would never put her suffering into words. She leaned close and held me tight, whispering: "Study hard. Live well. One of us must carry this family forward."

The train to Chengdu shrieked, its whistle cutting across the crowd. Smoke billowed, and the slogans rose with it: To the frontier! Build the new world! Voices cracked, some from pride, others from fear. A few wept quietly, turning their faces away.

When the train lurched forward, Wen Wen leaned out just once, lifted her hand, and waved. Only once. Then her figure dissolved into the smoke, swallowed by the westbound train.

I stood frozen on the platform, the echo of her touch still burning on my sleeve. I was too young then to grasp the full weight of that goodbye. All I knew was that my sister was gone, and that I had been left behind.

Later I would learn of the harshness of her journey—the military trucks, the endless mountain roads, the thin air that stole her breath. But on that morning, all I felt was the hollow of absence, the silence after the train had vanished, and the first true sense of what it meant to be separated by fate.

CHAPTER 13

The Road West

The true journey began after Chengdu.

There was no railway to Tibet then—only convoys of military trucks, canvas stretched taut to keep out the cold. Wen Wen and a dozen other youths crammed shoulder to shoulder on wooden benches, their bodies jostling with every turn.

At first, they sang to steady themselves. Some raised the International, their thin voices defiant against the engine's roar. Others shouted pledges of loyalty, declaring how they would build factories, villages, a new world at the frontier. Wen Wen did not join their shouting. She smiled faintly, listening, her thoughts hidden.

Soon the road silenced them. The climb was relentless, twisting high above churning rivers. Dust clogged their throats by day, by night, the cold pierced through every layer of cloth. When the truck jolted too hard, they clung to one another, laughter dissolving into groans.

For Wen Wen, the air itself became the enemy. Each breath grew thin, her chest rising shallowly. She was slighter than most, but never allowed herself to bend. She sat upright, her eyes fixed forward, as if refusing to let exhaustion see her falter.

During brief halts, the youths stumbled out, limbs trembling. Some squatted at the roadside, dizzy and retching. Others tried to rally the group: Think of the future we will build! Think of the new world ahead! Wen Wen listened quietly. Perhaps she wanted to believe them. Perhaps belief was the only shield they had.

At night, beneath the faint glow of a lantern, she opened her notebook and wrote: The road is long, the wind unkind, yet westward my heart must go.

I read those words years later. Even then, I could feel the weight of her silence between the lines—her fear, her longing, her refusal to give in.

The convoy rolled deeper into the mountains, carrying its fragile cargo of young lives. They had no idea what awaited them in Tibet. All they knew was that they were part of something vast, something larger than their own stories. And in that belief, they kept moving forward.

CHAPTER 14

Arrival in Chamdo

After endless days of jolting roads, the trucks finally crested onto the Tibetan plateau.

When the canvas flaps were thrown open, Wen Wen lifted her face to the light—and held her breath. Before her rose mountains like walls of heaven itself, peaks sharp and white, burning against a sky impossibly blue. Clouds drifted slowly, like sails on a boundless sea. The air was thin and raw, cutting into her lungs, yet also strangely pure.

Some of the youths cried out in wonder. Others shouted as if to prove they could match the grandeur of the peaks. Even in her weariness, Wen Wen felt a shiver of reverence, fear, and longing. She had never imagined the world could be so vast—or so unforgiving.

Chamdo itself offered no welcome. There were no finished factories, no warm houses waiting. Only a stretch of stony ground, a cluster of half-built sheds, and the endless sweep of mountains. Water and food were rationed. Nights froze them to the bone, even huddled together under thin blankets. Within weeks, hundreds more youths arrived from across China, each carrying the same slogans, the same forced hopes.

Labor began at once. They hauled stone, dug foundations, swung hammers until blisters split and bled. The loudspeakers shouted over them: Seize revolution, promote production! Fear no hardship, fear no death! When exhaustion knocked someone down, others dragged them back to their feet. No one dared fall behind.

But when night came, the sky filled with stars brighter than any they had ever known. Beneath that brilliance, the youths gathered outside their sheds. Some sang folk songs, some revolutionary anthems; the voices were cracked, but together they rose steady into the cold air. Wen Wen would sometimes open her notebook and told her team member stories she had memorized, her voice soft yet clear. The others leaned in, listening, their faces lit by firelight and by the fragile comfort of words.

In those nights, she became a quiet center. Not a leader by command, but a presence others sought when despair threatened to overtake them.

CHAPTER 15

Under the Stars

Nights in Chamdo carried a silence unlike any Wen Wen had known. The cold pressed in from every direction, sharp and insistent, yet above their heads the heavens opened with a brilliance that stole their breath. The stars spilled across the sky in rivers of light, so close it seemed one could reach out and pluck them.

After long days of breaking stones, mixing cement, and hauling timber, the youths would gather outside their crude dormitory sheds. Too tired to talk of politics, they spoke instead of home—of mothers cooking dumplings, of rivers they used to swim in, of classrooms now lost to chaos. Some fell quiet, eyes reflecting both longing and disbelief at how far they had come.

It was then that Wen Wen would open her notebook. She had carried it from home, its pages

55

filling slowly with copied passages, remembered stories, and her diary. By the dim glow of a kerosene lamp, she would read aloud—sometimes a tale from the old novels she once loved, sometimes simply her own thoughts shaped into gentle rhythm.

Her voice was soft, almost hesitant, but in the stillness of the plateau it carried. The others listened intently, their breathing slowing, their shoulders loosening. For a moment, the blisters and bruises, the hunger and fatigue, seemed to fade.

One night, when she paused, a young man murmured, "Keep going… your words make me forget the cold."

She smiled shyly and continued.

Sometimes others sang. Folk songs from their provinces mingled with revolutionary anthems, voices rising thin but determined into the night air. The songs were imperfect, cracked with weariness, but together they formed a chorus that reached toward the glittering sky.

Wen Wen slowly became the quiet center of these evenings. She never declared herself a leader, never raised her voice above the others. Yet it was to her that they turned when spirits sagged. Her stories, her calm, even her silence carried strength.

In those nights, beneath the stars, they became more than comrades-they became a family forged in hardship. And my sister, without ever meaning to, became their light.

CHAPTER 16

The Trial of the New Machines

Two years passed, measured not by calendars but by the slow rise of walls and the thickening of calluses on their hands. What had once been a barren field littered with timber and stone now stood as the rough outline of a factory. The roof beams stretched into place, the walls closed in, and the day came when the machines—those hulking masses of iron they had carried and bolted together—were ready for their first trial run.

The entire camp gathered, their faces weathered by wind and exhaustion but lit with expectation. Wen Wen stood among them—thin, her skin browned by the plateau sun, her hands cracked and rough, yet her eyes bright with that old stubborn flame.

The foreman gave a signal. With a shudder and a roar, the machines came alive. Metal teeth clashed, belts snapped into motion, and the sound shook the very ground. For a moment it was deafening, terrifying even—but then applause erupted. Some shouted, some cried outright, their voices rising above the grinding din. For them, that noise was more than mechanics; it was proof that their years of toil had not been swallowed by silence.

That night, the workers sang under the same cold stars. Their voices were hoarse, their throats raw, but the songs carried upward like sparks from a fire. Wen Wen later told me she sang with them, though her thoughts were divided. Pride filled her—how could it not, after so much pain? yet a quiet unease lingered. Could the birth of a factory truly repay the youth they had lost on the high plateau?

Soon after, word arrived: a handful of the most diligent workers would be chosen for further training in Shanghai. Wen Wen's name was among them.

When she told me in her next letter, I could almost see her handwriting quicken, her words straining against the page: "Maybe this is a door, maybe only a window. But if it opens, I must walk through it."

To Wen Wen, Shanghai was not merely a city - it was a glimpse of the life she might have lived if history had been kinder.

CHAPTER 17

Shanghai

For six months, Wen Wen lived in a world that seemed like a dream compared to the plateau.

The training was rigorous—long hours in chemical workshops, the sting of acid in the air, the endless repetition of technical drills. But beyond the factory gates stretched a city that dazzled her. Shanghai was alive with color and noise: the clang of trams, the tide of bicycles, the hum of shops spilling light across crowded streets. Compared to the gray mountains and skies of Tibet, it felt another world entirely.

In her letters, she tried to describe it to me. The fabrics in the shop windows glowed with impossible brightness—silks, cottons, the new synthetic cloths, patterns she had never seen. Most man still wore the familiar blue and gray, but some young women walked by in dresses of vivid color, their hair styled in the latest fashion. A few young men strode past in crisp shirt and polished shoes, their trousers cut like drumstick pants or flared bell-bottoms that had just come into style. My sister, in her plain work clothes, felt shy at first - but her curiosity was stronger than her shyness.

One afternoon, she wrote, she gathered her wages and bought a bolt of cloth—well-designed modern synthetic cotton. She carried it to a tailor and asked for two garments: a blouse and a dress. When she tried them on for the first time, standing before a mirror, she told me it was as if she had stepped into another version of herself. Not the girl bound to the plateau, but a young woman with her own grace.

She also spent money on me—my first set of "modern" clothes. Before the package arrived, I received her letter, with a small sketch of the shirt and trousers inside. I could almost feel her pride as she described them, imagining how I would look wearing them. Even from far away, she wanted to wrap me in dignity.

Before returning to Tibet, she and her friends had many photographs taken. In those pictures—kept in our family box—she stands by the Bund, at the shopping center, in front of museum, or near Fudan University. Her face was calm, her smile radiant, and her new dresses made her look truly beautiful. She mailed some of her photos home with a note:

"Dearest Mama and Brother, I am well. Shanghai is a place where even dreams walk the streets."

During that time, Aunt and Uncle came from Hangzhou to see her. They brought her steaming bowls of food, pressed money into her hands, and reminded her she was loved. Uncle told her softly:

"You may yet have a chance to go to university. There are new places opening for workers like you. Keep working, Wen Wen—don't give up."

Those words pierced her like a spark. In her notebook she wrote later: "Perhaps the door is not forever closed. If I am patient, maybe it will open again."

Shanghai had given her more that training or knowledge. It was proof that another life was possible, a life of books, of dignity, of dreams not yet buried. She carried that light with her, even as the train carried her west again.

CHAPTER 18

Return to Chamdo

The six months in Shanghai slipped away like a dream at dawn. Wen Wen folded her new dress carefully into the bottom of her bag, tucked the Bund photograph between the pages of her notebook, and boarded the train west.

The journey back was long. From the crowded coast through endless fields, and then, as the rails ended, onto the back of army trucks grinding up toward the plateau. She told me later how strange it felt: the nearer she drew to Tibet, the sharper the wind cut her face, and the thinner the air grew in her lungs. It was as though her body remembered too quickly what her spirit had wanted to forget.

The factory had changed. What had once been scaffolding and rubble was now a solid shape of walls and machines. Smoke trailed from chimneys; the clang of metal echoed against the mountains. The slogans were the same— "Grasp revolution, promote production!"—but now the black-ink characters on red paper hung inside the factory walls instead of bare foundations.

Wen Wen had changed, too. She was made a team leader, her thin frame carrying the weight of others' schedules and responsibilities. She guided her group through long shifts, her voice steady, her hands calloused. Yet beneath the authority, she carried something more private: the ember Shanghai had placed in her heart.

In her letters she wrote to me about it, never directly, but always between the lines. "If I work hard enough, perhaps there will be another chance. Perhaps the doors of the university are not closed forever."

At night, she sat beneath the vast, pitiless sky of the plateau, her notebook open on her knees. She would trace sentence she had written before leaving Shanghai: "Maybe the door is not forever closed." In those words, she found strength to rise each morning, to face the factory's roar.

I think of her often in that moment—my sister in the shadow of the mountains, clutching both the dream of Shanghai and the duty of the plateau. To the world she was a worker, a group leader, another nameless figure in the machinery of production. To me, she was something far rarer: a young woman who refused to surrender her hope, even when the air itself seemed too thin to breathe.

CHAPTER 19

Life on the Plateau

Life in Chamdo soon found its rhythm, though it was a rhythm of exhaustion. The days began before dawn with the clang of the factory bell and ended long after dusk when the last shift stumbled back to the dormitories.

Wen Wen became known not only for her hard work but also for the way she lifted others. She was chosen to help lead the factory's cultural team— singing at assemblies, teaching songs to weary workers in the evenings, and writing short essays to encourage everyone. After grueling shifts, when most collapsed onto their bunks, she would gather a few younger girls to prepare the next performance for the factory celebrations. Her voice was gentle, yet in the silence of the plateau it carried like a balm. Sometimes laughter would rise, thin but genuine, and echo softly against the cold dormitory walls.

But beneath that calm exterior, another story unfolded. Twice, her name appeared on the list of candidates for the coveted "worker-peasant-soldier" university slots. Twice she worked harder than anyone—filling out forms, practicing essays, holding onto the fragile dream of walking through the gates of a university. And twice the answer came back the same: rejected. *Political review failed*

The reason was never stated outright, but she knew. We all knew. Our parents' past clung to her like a shadow she could not shake. No amount of effort or devotion could wash away the mark of "reactionary" once written into a family record.

At night, when the others slept, she sat alone with her notebook. She wrote lines that trembled between defiance and despair, asking herself whether she still had the strength to fight for another chance:

I have tried my best to be excellent. I have given everything to the factory. Yet the gate remains closed. If my parents' names are chains, how can my heart ever be free?

She never read these words aloud. To her comrades, she was unshakable—someone to lean on, someone who brought light. To herself, she was a bird with clipped wings, singing to hide the pain of not being able to fly.

Only later did I realize how deeply those years on the plateau had shaped her. Outwardly, she was honored, trusted, admired. Inwardly, she bore a wound that never fully healed: the knowledge that no matter how hard she tried, the life she truly longed for—of books, of study, of freedom—remained just beyond reach.

CHAPTER 20

Shadows of an Accident

The pressure never eased. Each week the quotas rose, painted in fresh red across the factory walls: "More steel, more speed—grasp revolution, promote production!" The slogans were louder than the machines, but it was the machines that swallowed the workers' strength.

Many of those machines had been hauled across half of China, secondhand, patched together, already tired before they reached the plateau. Belts slipped, gears groaned, valves hissed steam through loose seals. Everyone saw the dangers, but no one dared slow the line. To speak of repairs was to risk being accused of laziness, of sabotage. "Later," the foremen always barked. "First finish the quota."

So accidents crept in like an unwelcome guest that refused to leave. A sleeve caught and torn away, a hand pulled into a belt, a worker fainting from fumes.

Once, a burst of oil flared into sudden flame, sending black smoke curling toward the rafters before it was beaten down. Each time, the injuries were dismissed as "minor issues," and the line resumed.

Wen Wen held herself steady, though I know now she must have been afraid. She tried to lead by example, to keep others calm. Yet in her letters, I could feel the weight between the lines—phrases clipped short, sentences ending in uneasy silence. She wrote of "tired days" and "machines that groan like old men."

Her friends whispered their fears at night. "We're pushing too fast," one confided. "The machines are hungry—they'll take someone whole if we're not careful." Another girl told Wen Wen, "My grandmother used to say: disasters are like dust. We think it is nothing, until the day it buries us."

Wen Wen didn't answer, but she remembered. Later she told me those words echoed in her head whenever the machines shrieked louder than usual.

The signs were all there—the fraying belts, the careless orders, the silence of workers who swallowed their fear. The shadow had already fallen across her path. None of us saw how close it was, or how swiftly it would strike.

CHAPTER 21

The Night of Explosion

It happened on a night shift. The air inside the factory was sharper than the cold outside, full of steam and metal dust. The machines hammered on, their rhythm uneven, like a heart about to fail.

That evening, one of the main engines shook harder than usual. Bolts rattled; gears ground against each other with a shrill whine. Some workers glanced at one another. Someone muttered, "It should be stopped." But the foreman snapped back, "No delays. Tonight's quota must be met!"

Wen Wen was among those on duty. She kept her eyes fixed on the machine, her jaw tight. Later I often wondered—did she sense what was coming? Did her body know before her mind could?

The moment came suddenly: a screech like tearing steel, then a violent jolt. The belt snapped free, whipping through the air like a furious lash.

Sparks burst from grinding gears. Then fire, shrapnel, chaos.

She was thrown to the floor. For an instant she saw only bursts of light, like a swarm of fireflies in the dark. Shouts and cries rang out, footsteps thundered, and the sharp scent of oil and blood filled the room.

When she looked down, her right hand lay not far from her body, and her arm was mangled beyond saving. She told me later she didn't feel pain at first, only the cold shock of absence, as though her body no longer belonged to her. Then the pain came, flooding in, drowning everything.

"Get her out!" voices shouted. She was lifted onto a makeshift stretcher, carried into the freezing night. Stars burned cruelly bright above, as if the heavens themselves were indifferent. The cold bit into her skin, but she was burning from within, her blood pouring out faster than anyone could stop.

She slipped into darkness.

When she woke again, it was to the white glare of hospital walls and the acrid sting of disinfectant. She turned her head and saw the bandages—saw what was no longer there. Her right arm, the hand that had written poems, the hand that had turned pages, was gone.

She lay still, staring at the ceiling, silent for hours. When others came to comfort her, she could not listen. Finally, she whispered to no one in particular:

"How can I write? How can I live now?"

I wasn't there. But when the letter came—when I learned what she had lost—it felt as if the explosion had reached across the plateau and struck me too.

CHAPTER 22

A Letter-Words in Reverse

The weeks after the accident blurred into silence. Wen Wen lay in the infirmary, pale against the white sheets even after multiple transfusion, her right arm wrapped in thick layers of bandages. Breathing was heavy work in the thin air; healing came slower still. Each day others with minor injuries passed by her door, returning to work. She envied them—not the toil, but the simple grace of movement: to rise, to reach, to care for oneself without help.

What tormented her most was not the physical pain, but the thought of us at home. She did not know how to tell our mother and me about her injury, and she could not bear the thought of adding to our father's pain - he had only just been released from prison.

So, one evening, still weak, she asked for paper. Propping herself up, she took the pen awkwardly in her left hand. The letters came out crooked, tilting sideways, as though each stroke fought against gravity. Her hand shook; her lips pressed tight. Still, she forced herself on.

The letter was short.

Dear Brother,

How are you? I am fine here, don't worry. Our work continues. My right hand was slightly injured, so I'm using my left hand to write to you today. Please tell Father and Mother I think of them every day, and that I'll write to them soon.

At the end she added, her writing more faltering than before: "Sometimes the nights feel long. I wonder where the road will lead. But I know you are studying hard. That gives me comfort, and pride. Write back soon. Wen Wen."

When the ink dried, the page looked strange— slanted lines, unbalanced strokes, as if the words had been reflected in a mirror. She folded it carefully, as though the fragile paper carried her entire will to survive.

Weeks later, the letter reached us. I remember holding it in my hands, tracing the uneven characters. They were not the graceful script I had grown up admiring. They bore something heavier—pain, endurance, and silence.

I showed my sister's letter to our parents. Mother whispered, "This is her hand... but not her hand." Father said nothing, but I caught the flicker of fear in his eyes. We all knew something had happened, something she hadn't written.

For me, it was the first time I truly feared that my sister's life had changed forever, though the full truth we learned only later.

CHAPTER 23

Echoes of Home

Two weeks passed after Wen Wen's first letter—
the one she had written to me alone, shaky and
uneven, telling me not to worry. We waited anxiously
for more news, and then at last, a second letter
arrived. This time it was addressed to all of us.

The envelope was worn from travel, the paper
inside carrying the faint scent of distance. We
gathered in our parent's kitchen as Mother unfolded
it.

Her voice trembled as she read:

"Dearest parents and brother, I am well. Do not
worry. My right hand is not as it was, so my left-hand
writing is clumsy. But I think of you every day, and I
hold your faces in my heart."

The handwriting wavered across the page,
crooked and strained. Mother stopped, whispering,

"She's injured her right hand...but she didn't tell us how badly." Her fingers lingered on the paper, as though trying to read what Wen Wen had chosen not to write.

Father stared long and hard before speaking. "If something unbearable has happened, she would never tell us in a letter. She has always tried to carry pain alone." His words were steady, but his eyes were shadowed.

I felt it too—that unspoken truth in the tilted strokes.

Only a few months earlier, Father had been released from prison. Last month, he was reinstated at the university. His honor was restored, his name cleared—he was even appointed president of the college. After years of disgrace, our home had begun to breathe again.

Mother said, "We must write back at once. She needs to know the shadows over our family are gone. She must know she can come home -we haven't seen her for years."

So together we composed our reply.

Mother wrote first: "Dearest Wen Wen, we miss you deeply and long to see you soon.". Father added his line, his hand firm: "I have returned to the university. My name is clear, my position restored. You are our beloved daughter. I hope I can do something to help you."

And I, the younger brother she had once cared for and urged to study hard, wrote: "Sister, we are worried. Please be strong. If you cannot return by yourself, I will come to bring you home."

When the letter was finished, Father pressed his official stamp beneath his name, as though to make the truth undeniable. Mother slipped a sprig of dried jasmine inside. "So she will smell home," she murmured.

We sent it off, though the unease never left us. That night, Mother whispered to me, "She is suffering - I can feel it. When she reads this, perhaps she will finally let us bring her home."

In the weeks that followed, every knock on the door, every postman's step, made our hearts quicken. We were waiting - not just her reply, but for her return home.

CHAPTER 24

The Call of Home Coming

Her second letter had unsettled us, but our reply—Father's restored honor, Mother's tenderness, my promise—set out across the mountains, carrying with it a sprig of jasmine pressed between the pages. Weeks later, Wen Wen finally received it.

I picture her then, sitting on her narrow cot in the workers' dormitory, the pale light of the plateau falling across her face. When she opened the envelope, the dry scent of jasmine rose to her, faint but unmistakable. She trembled as she unfolded the pages.

The first words were Mother's: "We missed you deeply. You are never alone. Whatever pain you carry, we will carry it with you." Wen Wen told me later that her tears came before she could read further.

Then came Father's firm script, followed by my offer to bring her home. She pressed the pages to her chest, as though the weight of those words might hold her together.

Wen Wen wept openly then, clutching the letter until her knuckles whitened. For the first time since the accident, she allowed herself to believe that the shame she bore need not be hers alone—that the chains binding her might at last be loosening.

That night, she did not sleep. She stared at the ceiling, whispering again and again, "I must go home. Only there can I truly heal."

The next morning, she summoned her strength and wrote a petition to the factory leadership. Her left hand moved slowly, but the meaning was clear: "Because of my injury, I cannot recover properly here. I beg permission to return to my parents' city for treatment and rest. Once well, I will accept any assignment."

For days she waited in dread. If they refused, she would remain exiled, half-whole, struggling against silence. But the answer came back with unexpected mercy: approval. "Go home and recover," they told her. "Later, we will see what work you can do."

So she began to pack. Her belongings were few: the dress she had bought in Shanghai, the notebook whose pages were now filled with uneven lines, and the letters from us—folded and refolded until the creases were worn thin.

When the truck finally rumbled out of Chamdo, carrying her down from the high plateau, she looked back once at the distant snow peaks. They had been her prison and her crucible. Now they faded behind her, while her heart raced with every mile—because the road, at last, was leading her home.

CHAPTER 25

Reunion

The journey home was long, but to Wen Wen it must have felt like a dream slowly taking shape. Each station, each passing town carried her closer to the city she had pictured through years of exile. By the time the train pulled into the station, her heart must have been racing too fast to steady.

I remember that day clearly. We stood on the crowded platform—Father in his formal jacket, Mother clutching a handkerchief, and I, taller and stronger now, trying to appear calm though my palms were damp with sweat.

And then she stepped down.

Wen Wen was thinner than I remembered, her face lined by hardship, yet her posture still carried its quiet poise. For a heartbeat she stood motionless, a bag slung across her shoulder, as though afraid the sight of us might dissolve if she moved.

I could not wait. I rushed forward and gripped her left arm—the one that remained—holding it as if I could keep her from slipping away.

"Jiejie!" My voice cracked.

Mother followed close behind, tears streaming as her hands moved over Wen Wen's shoulders, her hair, her face—touching as though to confirm she was truly there. "My child, my good girl…" The words broke into sobs.

Father came last. His eyes, sharp as ever, fell on the empty sleeve. He did not cry. Instead, he turned aside, polishing his glasses before slipping them back on. When he faced her again, his voice was steady:

"You are home. That is what matters."

We brought her to the new house the university had assigned Father after his reinstatement. It was bright, spacious, lined with books once more. Yet even there, a quiet weight filled the air. At dinner we spoke of journey, her health, of changes in the city, of my preparation for university applications—but not of the accident. That silence said more than words could.

That night, in her old room, she unpacked her few belongings: the Shanghai dress folded neatly, the battered notebooks and our letters, worn from being unfolded too often. She laid them on the desk like talismans. When she lay down, the sounds of home surrounded her—Mother closing the kitchen door, Father pacing in his study, my pages turning in the next room. After so many years of dust and fear, safety wrapped itself around her at last.

But safety did not erase silence.

Life after Wen Wen's return was at once ordinary and fragile, like porcelain carefully set on a shelf. On the surface, everything seemed restored: Father walked the university halls again, now as its president; Mother moved through the house with renewed purpose, tending to students and colleagues who came to visit; and I, balancing factory duties with preparation for the university entrance exams, buried my head in books.

Yet the center of our home was Wen Wen.

She could no longer work as she once had, yet she refused to be idle. She read widely from Father's library. With her left hand she practiced writing until her script, though never as elegant as before, grew steadier. She helped Mother with chores, folded laundry, even insisted on carrying small baskets from the market. When neighbors came, she greeted them with calm dignity, never letting her empty sleeve speak before she did.

At night, I would sometimes hear her in her room, quietly turning pages of a book, or humming a tune she had once sung with her workmates in Tibet. Her voice was softer now, but it carried a warmth that filled the house.

Still, I knew the silence weighed on her. She rarely spoke of the factory, the accident, or the long years away. Only once did she say, in a low voice meant more for herself than for me:

"The world I dreamed of is gone. But I can still make a world here, for you, for Mama, for Baba."

It was in those words that I understood her strength—not the strength of achievement or recognition, but the quiet strength of choosing to keep living, to keep giving, even when so much had been taken.

In those days, our family seemed whole again. We had never been so close, nor loved one another so deeply. And at the heart of that fragile peace was my sister Wounded yet unyielding- who held us together.

CHAPTER 26

The Belated Letter

Days at home passed in comfort. Wen Wen grew stronger, yet her thoughts often drifted elsewhere. Each evening, after the lamps were dimmed, I could see her gaze lingering on the shadows, her silence carrying the weight of someone far away. I knew she was thinking of him—Da Chuan. She had once told me about his laughter, the way he played the erhu with such quiet intensity, the letters he had written when she was barred from university, promising that no matter what, he wished her to be his lifelong companion.

Now, in our parents' house, surrounded by safety, what pained her most was not her arm, but his silence.

One night she sat at her desk, the old notebook open before her, its blank pages waiting. I learned later what she wrote that evening, slowly and awkwardly with her left hand:

"Da Chuan,

It has been too long since I last wrote. I must tell you the truth. I was injured in the factory. My right hand… is gone. I am learning to live independently again, but it is hard. Sometimes the nights feel endless. Still, I hold on. I am with my family now. My father has been restored to his post, and my brother is about to begin university.

You once told me music gave you strength in hardship. I now search for words to do the same.

I do not know what the future holds for us. Yet I hope you will not forget me. Write to me, even if only a few words.

Wen Wen"

When her letter was sealed and sent, she waited with a restlessness that filled the house. At meals she tried to seem calm, but I noticed her glancing toward the gate whenever footsteps passed.

At last, his reply arrived. She showed it to me, her hands trembling.

"Wen Wen,

I am glad to receive your letter. Thank you for telling me the truth about your injury. I have been promoted; my future in the army looks bright. For now, you must focus on your recovery. As for personal matters, I must first consult my parents. I am their only son, and their opinion carries great weight. Let us stay in touch.

Da Chuan"

She read those lines again and again, but the distance between them only grew wider. I could see the sorrow in her face, though she tried to hide it.

Not long after, another letter came—this time colder, final:

"Wen Wen,

I have spoken with my parents. For my career and for their peace of mind, I must follow their wishes. They hope I will marry the daughter of an old comrade, from a respected military family. I am sorry, but I cannot refuse them. You will always have my respect. I wish you healthier and happy.

—Da Chuan"

That night, Wen Wen did not sleep. I found her the next morning with swollen eyes. She forced a smile and whispered, "Perhaps this is for the best. I don't want to be a burden to anyone."

Later, our mother took her left hand, her voice both gentle and firm:

"Child, if he cannot stand with you now, he never will. Love must give strength, not pity."

Wen Wen nodded, but I knew the wound went deeper than words could reach. In the weeks that followed, she returned to her books, her silence heavier but steadier. A scar had formed—one that time would never truly erase.

CHAPTER 27

The Proposal

After Da Chuan's last letter, our home grew quieter. None of us spoke of him again, though the silence itself was full of his absence. Yet our parents soon began to worry about Wen Wen's future- her work, her health, her happiness, her life.

One evening Father said, "It may be better for her to meet someone. She deserves a companion she can rely on."

Mother agreed, though she knew the search would not be simple. Wen Wen's injury might cause hesitation, yet they believed dignity and kindness mattered more than appearances.

Suggestions soon came from friends and neighbors: "A young teacher at the middle school— kind, from a good family." Another said, "A doctor, well-educated and stable. He would surely treat her well."

Doctors and teachers were still among the most respected professions in those days-matches considered steady, honorable, and safe. To our parents, such a proposal seems promising: a path toward stability and care.

One autumn afternoon, I watched as our mother sat with Wen Wen in the courtyard. Dry leaves skittered across the ground, the air turning chill. Gently, she said:

"Wen Wen, you have endured much, missed chances because of us. But you are still young. You deserve a home of your own. We have spoken with friends. Would you mind meeting someone?"

Wen Wen lowered her eyes to her left hand—the one that still served her, the right folded into its empty sleeve. After a long pause, she whispered:

"If it eases your hearts, I will meet him. But I ask only this: that he be someone who respects me."

Our mother's eyes filled with tears. "That is all we want—for you to be loved."

Not long after, an introduction was arranged. The man was a surgeon at the city hospital. He had been married once before, divorced soon after. In those years, divorce left a stain, yet when our parents met him, they found him steady, intelligent, and respectful.

For the first time in months, it seemed a door had opened—narrow, uncertain, but real. Wen Wen prepared herself to step through, though in her heart the scars of love and loss had not yet healed.

CHAPTER 28

First Meeting

It was a Sunday afternoon, quiet and cool, when my parents asked Wen Wen to attend the arranged meeting. Mother laid out a simple but modest dress for her, smoothing the collar with gentle hands. The fabric shimmered softly in the light—elegant yet unassuming.

"You look beautiful," Mother whispered. Wen Wen gave a faint smile, though I could see the unease in her eyes.

We went together to a colleague's home, where the meeting was arranged. When the door opened, I saw him for the first time: tall, broad-shouldered, with the steady bearing of a man accustomed to responsibility. His face was serious, almost stern, though not without composure.

"This is Dr. Huang," our host introduced. "He works at the city hospital."

The doctor extended his hand politely. "It is an honor to meet you, Comrade Wen Wen." His voice was formal, his grip firm.

After a brief exchange of pleasantries, our mutual friend and I withdrew to another room, leaving the two of them seated across from each other in the small parlor, teacups neatly placed before them.

At first, the conversation was cautious: her recovery, her planned transfer to a nearby middle school library, his long hours at the hospital and potential promotion. Wen Wen spoke softly, eyes lowered, while Dr. Huang spoke at length about surgeries performed, patients saved, and the demands of his profession.

To those watching from outside, it looked promising: a respected doctor, a modest young woman. She listened carefully, nodding. He had not asked about her dreams or her joys—only about himself, his accomplishments, his reputation.

Still, she remained polite. That was her way, and our parents' hopes weighed heavily on her. She smiled faintly when expected, her silence mistaken for admiration.

When the meeting ended, Dr. Huang bowed slightly. "You are a remarkable young woman. I would be glad to see you again."

When we got home, Mother asked gently, "What do you think, child?"

Wen Wen hesitated. "He is respectable. Serious. Perhaps too serious." She lowered her voice. "But I cannot ask for much."

Mother held her hand. "We only want you to be cherished."

That night, I passed her room and saw her sitting at her desk, staring at the blank page of her notebook. The memory of Da Chuan's laughter, of Ji Chang's poems, must have lingered in her mind. She sighed and closed the cover. The past was gone. A new, restrained path lay before her.

CHAPTER 29

A New Post, A New Path

Before Wen Wen left Tibet, the factory leadership had given her three options: remain at the factory in a lighter role, retire early with a modest allowance, or request a transfer back inland for rehabilitation.

She was not yet thirty. To retire was to surrender; to return to the factory that had taken her arm was impossible. After long talks with our parents, she chose the third path: to return home and begin again.

Through Father's colleagues, news reached the principal of a local middle school that a librarian was needed. The man, who had once admired Father's scholarship, welcomed the idea. "She is educated, diligent, and disciplined," he said. "This position will suit her perfectly."

And so Wen Wen entered the school library and began a new life. I often watched her from the corner when I visited after work. With her left hand she arranged books—slowly, carefully. Students admired her patience and soft voice; teachers praised her meticulous notes in the catalog. Soon people spoke of her with respect:

"A young woman who has suffered hardship yet serves with dignity."

For Wen Wen, the library became a sanctuary. Surrounded by books, she recovered not only her body but her spirit. She was no longer a victim, but once again part of her community.

In this steadier state, she continued to see Dr. Huang. Their meetings remained formal, yet she faced them with more composure. "At least," she confided once, "I am not empty-handed. I can work. I can live independently."

Gradually, Dr. Huang brought her to meet his parents. They were ordinary working people—his mother worn by years of factory labor, his father gruff and silent. They could not ignore her disability; doubt was plain in their eyes. Yet they also understood our family's standing in the city. To them, this marriage promised both stability and advantage. In the end, they gave their consent.

Not long after, Dr. Huang came formally to our home. In the parlor, before our parents, he asked for her hand. I stood quietly by as Wen Wen lifted her eyes, saw the hope in our parents' faces, and answered softly: "Yes. I agree."

Thus the engagement was set.

CHAPTER 30

The Wedding

The library had become Wen Wen's refuge, her daily rhythm of books and students restoring a sense of belonging. And it was in those months of quiet healing that her engagement with Dr. Huang ripened into marriage.

The ceremony was to be modest, as was the custom then—no grand banquets, no extravagance. Still, our parents prepared carefully.

On the morning of the wedding, a clear and beautiful weekend day, Mother laid out a special garment. It had once been her own cherished cheongsam, preserved through the storms of revolution. Altered into a modern dress, it fit Wen Wen perfectly. The fabric gleamed softly, elegant yet restrained—carrying both the weight of the past and the hope of a new beginning.

"You look radiant," Mother whispered, fastening the last button. Wen Wen caught her reflection in the mirror: a young woman standing tall, though her sleeve hung empty. For a moment she paused and remembered the loved time and the laughter she once shared with friends long gone. Then she lowered her eyes and whispered back, "Thank you, Mother."

The ceremony was held in a simple hall at the hospital. Colleagues of Dr. Huang nodded approvingly; relatives offered congratulations. Wen Wen smiled politely, her calm composure concealing the storm within.

I stood beside her throughout, quietly protective. At one moment I leaned close and murmured, "Jiejie, whatever happens, we will always love you-you are not alone." I felt her hand tighten slightly at my words, and I knew they meant more than any formal blessing.

That night, when the celebrations were over, Wen Wen sat by the window of her new home. The city outside lay hushed; moonlight spilled across the floor. She touched the silk of her dress, her fingers brushing the emptiness of her sleeve.

This is her path now, I thought. Not chosen wholly with joy, but with resolve. And perhaps—though she did not yet believe it—in time she might find peace.

CHAPTER 31

New Life

At first, Wen Wen's married life unfolded with a kind of fragile order. Each morning, she tidied their small apartment, then walked to the school library, where the familiar scent of books seemed to steady her. In the evenings she prepared meals with quiet care, learning to chop and stir one-handed, never allowing frustration to show.

When they visited Dr. Huang's parents together, Wen Wen always behaved with respect—bowing slightly, answering their questions with patient, helping with small chores. She noticed that her father-in-law spoke sharply to his wife, always in a tone of command, while his mother-in-law gossiped restlessly and never failed to ask when a grandchild would arrive. Wen Wen would smile faintly and endure.

At home, her life with Dr. Huang was steady— perhaps too steady. He was serious, often absent, his mind consumed by the hospital. When he was there, he spoke of surgeries and promotions, his words heavy with ambition. Wen Wen listened patiently, nodding as though impressed. But he rarely asked about her work, or her thoughts.

For a time, she told herself this must be what marriage was—two lives running in parallel, rarely intersecting. She accepted the silences at the dinner table, the late nights he came home smelling faintly of alcohol, the way he sank into bed without a word.

Yet unease grew. His patient thinned. He began to complain about her slow movement or scold her for misplacing a dish. Once, when she left papers scattered on the desk, he gathered them roughly and said, "You should not trouble yourself with writing. Focus on the home."

That night, Wen Wen sat alone, the crumpled paper in her lap. She did not weep, but she felt the first true crack in this new life.

Still, she pressed on. In the library, among rows of books and the eager voices of children, she found solace. Their questions, their laughter, reminded her that tenderness still existed in the world. When I visited her, she always spoke of the bright moments- new students, kind colleagues, the joy of reading a new book. Yet I sensed, even between her cheerful lines, the peace she tried so hard to build was fragile; like glass perched too close to the edge of a table— any sudden jolt, and it might shatter.

CHAPTER 32

The Fracture

The first year and half of her marriage passed in a blur of routine. The library gave Wen Wen a sense of purpose, the apartment, a sense of confinement.

Outwardly, Dr. Huang was dutiful. His reputation at the hospital grew; colleagues praised him as a surgeon. But at home, his temper shortened. When he returned late, weary from long shifts, he drank quietly, his words clipped and sharp.

At first it was small things: a dish too salty, a shirt not ironed well enough. Wen Wen, patient as ever, endured it, telling herself, He is tired. He carries burdens I cannot see. But the discontent deepened. One evening, after midnight, he came home reeking of alcohol. Wen Wen rose to greet him, relieved only that he was safe. She asked gently, "Would you like some tea?"

His reply was a snap: "Why fuss over useless things? Can't you see I'm exhausted?"

Before the words had even faded, his hand struck her cheek. The sound cracked through the small room. Wen Wen froze, her face burning, her heart pounding like a drum. She stared in disbelief. The man she had once trusted had truly struck her.

Silence followed. Dr. Huang muttered something about stress, about her nagging, then collapsed onto the bed, asleep within minutes. Wen Wen stood by the window, her hand on her cheek. Outside, the city lay in darkness, a pale moon breaking through the clouds. Tears slid down her face, but she did not sob. Instead, she whispered to herself, *I chose this path. I must endure.*

The next morning, she dabbed powder over the faint mark and went to the library as usual. The students ran to her, asking for book recommendations, their voices bright and innocent. She continued arranging bookshelves, listing new journals on blackboard, answering questions from teachers and students. No one could see the storm inside her.

It was the first fracture—but not the last.

CHAPTER 33

Endurance and Cracks

That slap was only the beginning. After that night, storms came in waves—sometimes fierce, sometimes faint, but never gone. Harsh words became daily; raised hands followed when anger spilled over. To the neighbors, their home seemed quiet. Behind the door, Wen Wen bore the silence of bruises, hidden under long sleeves and careful smiles.

And then—light in the darkness. Wen Wen discovered she was pregnant. The news filled her with fear and hope both. Fear—because she wondered if Dr. Huang could ever be the father her child needed. Hope—because a child meant renewal, a reason to endure.

Mother wept with joy and embraced Wen Wen. "With a child," she said, "your days will be full again, filled with laughter and joy." Our parents even began suggesting names for the unborn baby. Dr. Huang's family was equally elated. Her mother-in-law clapped in delight, speaking endlessly of the long-awaited grandchild. For the first time, Wen Wen felt less like a burden and more like a promise.

The pregnancy was hard. Morning sickness drained her, and her body—already weakened by years of hardship—grew frail. Dr. Huang showed little patience. "Other women work until the day they give birth," he snapped once. Still, Wen Wen pressed on—cooking, cleaning, shelving books at the library—until exhaustion forced her to stop.

When her son was born, Wen Wen's love was fierce enough to burn away every shadow. She held him close, kissed his small face, and whispered, "You are my hope. My tomorrow."

For a short time, even her husband seemed changed. He stood taller, proud of his son, showing him off to colleagues. Wen Wen allowed herself to dream—perhaps this child would soften him, perhaps the storms would pass.

But the old patterns soon returned: long nights away, the smell of alcohol, sharp criticism that turned again to blows. Life became a cycle of hurt and apology. Almost without fail, the next day he would mutter, eyes lowered, "I lost control. Forgive me. I am under pressure."

At first, Wen Wen wanted to believe him. She told herself tomorrow would be better. But the cycle repeated: uneasy calm, sudden storm, remorse, contrition. She began to feel like a bird in a cage—each time the door seemed to open; it slammed shut again.

She thought of leaving. More than once, she whispered over her son's sleeping form, I could take him and return to Father and Mother. We could begin anew. But reality crushed the thought. Divorce in those years meant disgrace—not only for her, but for both families.

So she stayed.

Her son became her anchor. His smile was her refuge; his small arms around her neck gave her courage to face another day. His first words, his first steps—those joys almost erased the bruises hidden beneath her sleeves.

And yet, beneath even that fragile joy, fear never left her. Each raised voice made her body tense; each apology rang emptier than the last. Deep inside, she knew: the cracks were only widening.

CHAPTER 34

An Island of the soul

Wen Wen's days soon fell into a rhythm. Each morning, she dressed her little boy, took his hand, and walked him to kindergarten. She lingered at the gate until he vanished into the crowd of children, then turned back toward the library.

There, routine gave her a measure of calm. She arranged books, answered questions, guided students with patience. Sometimes, in rare quiet moments, she opened a novel or a collection of essays, reading a few pages in silence. Books remained the only place where she felt free—though even that freedom had become cautious, hidden between her duties.

At home, things were different. She no longer dared to read. Her husband's eyes followed her every movement, and she had learned that even the sight of her holding a book could provoke his temper. So the volumes stayed closed, gathering dust, their silence as heavy as her own.

Her world shrank to three points on a map: the kindergarten gate, the library shelves, and the small apartment where shadows lengthened each night. Only her son's smile pierced the grayness. When he tugged her hand and laughed, warmth flickered across her face. For him she endured, for him she kept going.

Then came the whispers. Rumors of her husband's closeness with a young nurse, of long evenings at the hospital that had little to do with patients. At first, Wen Wen brushed them aside. He is busy. He works hard. People gossip.

But the signs became too clear. His absences grew longer, his excuses thinner. The faint scent of perfume clung to his clothes. When he came home, his gaze no longer sought hers, his words edged with impatience.

She felt the distance like a cold wind moving through her life. Yet she said nothing. Confrontation, she feared, would invite only another storm. Instead, she turned inward, blaming herself. *If only I were stronger. If I were prettier. If I had not lost my hand... perhaps he would not have turned away.*

The self-blame gnawed at her, deepening shadows already heavy in her mind. Where others might have raged, Wen Wen folded into silence. Each day she moved through her tasks—kindergarten drop-off, library shelves, meals at home—as though she lived behind glass, watching her own life from the outside.

Our parents noticed her pallor, the tremor in her voice. When I visited, I sensed a heaviness she would not name. But Wen Wen smiled faintly, insisting she was fine. She hid the bruises, the tears, the betrayal that hollowed her heart.

At night, when her son slept beside her, she lay awake staring at the ceiling. *What did I do wrong? Where did I fail?* The questions circled endlessly, with no answers—only the echo of her own blame.

She was no longer simply lonely. She was becoming an island, cut off from every shore.

And still the storms did not cease. Betrayal now entered openly, widening the gulf until I feared her spirit would collapse.

CHAPTER 35

On the Edge of Collapse

Years of storms, apologies, and silence had hollowed my sister's spirit. What began as sharp tempers and sudden blows had hardened into a shadow she carried everywhere. And now betrayal had entered too—the whispers of another woman, the coldness in her husband's eyes. Anger and abandonment pressed down together, unbearable in their weight.

To outsiders, her life seemed steady. Each morning, she walked her son to kindergarten; each afternoon she worked dutifully at the library; each evening she kept the household in order. Sleep no longer came easily. She often lay awake long after midnight, her thoughts circling endlessly—echoes of her husband's coldness, fragments of lost dreams, the constant question of where she had gone wrong. When she did sleep, it was shallow, haunted by anxious visions.

By day, she moved carefully, almost mechanically smiling when spoken to, nodding when asked questions. Her colleagues noticed her pallor and dim. distant eyes but thought she was simply tired.

Our parents, worn down by years of hardship, mistook her silence for obedience. Once, they gently asked about her marriage and relationship with her in-laws, but Wen Wen, not wanting to worry them, smiled faintly and said everything at home was fine-she was just tired. Mother urged her to get a check-up and invited her family to visit more often for meals. Wen Wen agreed, promising she would.

Even I, who loved her most, sometimes believed her faint smile was resilience. None of us saw how often she held her breath just to keep the tears from spilling.

Her son remained her only refuge. She poured what strength she had left into him, watching his face intently as though to memorize every detail. His laughter was still her light, but even that light could not fully chase away the shadows. Sometimes, when he slept beside her, she touched his small hand and whispered, I must endure. For you, I must endure. But her voice trembled, for she knew her strength was fraying, the thread thinning.

One evening, standing before the mirror, she barely recognized the hollow-eyed woman staring back. She looked older than her years, her face etched with sorrow no apology could erase. She was standing at the edge, and she knew it: one more storm, one more betrayal, one more night of unbearable silence—and the fragile balance would break.

And yet, a few fragile supports remained—our parents, me, her little boy. Threads she clung to, even as the ground gave way beneath her feet.

CHAPTER 36

The Last Supports

My sister clung to what little light remained.

Our parents, though aging, still offered her gentle words whenever she visited with her son. Mother would press her hand and say softly, "My child, tell us what we can do to help you. No matter how heavy the burden, you are not alone."

Father, quieter now than in his younger years, looked at her with weary eyes—eyes that carried both sorrow and pride. More than once, he asked carefully if she might speak with a counselor or family expert, hoping it could ease her pain. Yet even as he spoke, I could see his own helpless. He often felt guilty - for the lost years, for the opportunities his children had missed because of his political past.

Our parents sensed something deeper was wrong, but they could not reach the truth. Whenever they met with Wen Wen and Dr. Huang, both put on the appearance of harmony - speaking gently, pretending affection that had long faded.

I, busy with my own studies and work, came whenever I could. Over tea, I asked about her health, about the library, about her boy's lessons. Wen Wen always answered calmly, never revealing the storms inside her. To me she showed only a faint smile, as if protecting me from her pain, she could protect herself as well.

Her son was her truest anchor. He had grown from a timid toddler into a curious schoolboy, forever bringing home drawings and songs, tugging at her sleeve: Mama, look! In those moments, warmth returned to her face. She poured all her tenderness into him, silently praying that he might live the freedom she had lost.

And yet I sensed how fragile these supports were. The betrayals, the silences, the bruises hidden beneath her sleeve—none of them could be spoken aloud. At night she lay beside a man whose heart was elsewhere, blaming herself for what had been done to her. By day she endured with quiet dignity. By night she carried the weight alone.

The thread binding her to this world was thinning, and one more storm might break it. The storm came soon after, in Shanghai.

CHAPTER 37

The Breaking Point

It was Wen Wen who first spoke of Shanghai.

For weeks she had carried the thought quietly, like a secret ember. She remembered her training there years ago—the bustling streets, the bookstores, the walks along the Bund with her aunt and uncle. In Shanghai she had once felt alive, even hopeful. Perhaps, she thought, if she returned, she might recapture a fragment of that warmth—or at least breathe more freely for a few days.

One evening she gathered her courage and told her husband.
"I would like to visit Shanghai during the holiday," she said softly. "Just for a short while. To see the city again."

To her surprise, he agreed almost too quickly. "Yes," he said. "We can go."

She did not know then that he had his own reasons. When they arrived, the city glittered as always—crowds pressed through Nanjing Road, neon lights painted the night, trams clattered past. Yet for Wen Wen, the colors seemed muted, the joy distant. She walked the familiar streets, but the excitement she remembered no longer stirred in her chest.

On the third evening, after dinner back in the small hotel room, he spoke with the cold finality of a verdict. "We should separate," he said. "I don't think we belong together anymore. You're holding me back. I must think of my future." Wen Wen froze.

"As for the child," he continued, "he will stay with my parents. He is a member of the Huang family. They will raise him well. You may visit sometimes. When we return, we should arrange the divorce right away. It will be best for everyone."

Those words cut deeper than any blow. She had heard the rumors about the young nurse and had tried to dismiss her suspicions, but now the truth lay bare: he had already chosen a life that left no place for her.

Her lips parted, but no sound came. Inside, her heart screamed: My child is mine. You can't take him. I have given everything. Yet her voice failed.

Her husband turned away, satisfied with her silence. For him the matter was closed. That night Wen Wen tossed and turned, awake to the sounds of the city outside—the trams, a faint music, the laughter of passing couples. Once she had imagined Shanghai as a place of freedom; now it was the backdrop to her undoing.

Her last support—the bond with her son—was being stripped from her. Without him, without hope, she could see no reason to continue.

The breaking point had come. And it did not arrive quietly, but at a crowded train station where smoke and steam would soon hide the final choice she was forced to make.

CHAPTER 38

The Station

The return journey was heavy with silence.

They had left Shanghai early, her husband urging haste—he had shifts waiting at the hospital, a life to resume. The train they boarded was one of the old green carriages, coal smoke billowing thick across the platforms, the air dense with soot and steam. Passengers pushed and shouted, clutching their bundles, desperate to claim a seat.

At the transfer station, the chaos was worse. People surged forward as soon as the gates opened, running to secure a place. The air reeked of coal and sweat. Overhead, a locomotive shrieked, its whistle long and piercing, echoing through Wen Wen's chest like a summons.

Her husband told her he would go inside to buy food and water.

"Wait here," he said, pointing to a patch of platform

near the edge. "When the train comes, we'll get on together."

She nodded, standing still as the crowd pressed around her. Alone for the first time in days, she felt the ground tilt beneath her.

The noise of the station blurred—the shouting, the clatter of wheels, the hiss of steam. She heard instead another voice, faint yet insistent: the whisper of all her disappointments, her lost dreams, the betrayals she had endured. The whistle sounded again, sharp as a blade, and in it she heard her own thoughts: It is time. There is no other way.

For an instant, she saw herself as if from afar: a woman still young yet worn thin by sorrow; a mother whose child was being taken from her; a daughter who had tried to be good yet could not save her family; a wife who had given everything yet was cast aside.

Her eyes burned. She thought of her son, his small hand clutching hers at the kindergarten gate, his innocent voice calling, Mama, don't be late. A sob rose in her throat. Forgive me, she whispered inwardly. I am too tired. I cannot fight anymore. Perhaps in another life, I will find peace.

The whistle shrieked once more.

Her feet moved almost without command. Step by step, she drifted forward, her body swallowed by the steam, her figure blurring in the smoke and the press of the crowd. No one noticed—just another passenger carried along by the tide—until the scream of brakes tore through the station.

The world roared, then fell silent. The silence reached us like thunder.

CHAPTER 39

Aftermath

The news shattered our family.

Our parents aged ten years overnight. Mother's hair turned white in weeks; Father's shoulders stooped under a weight he could not lay down. At night they whispered, "If only we had protected her more."

Yet in their grief they made one firm choice: her son would not be surrendered to the Huang family. With the weight of their name and the help of old colleagues, they fought and secured the right to raise him themselves.

The boy clung to them, confused. "Where is Mama? Did she stop loving me?" They told him gently, "Your mother loved you more than anyone. She is watching over you from the sky." They poured all their love into him, though they knew the absence could never be filled.

For me, the news was like a blade to the chest. For years I could not speak her name. Each time it rose to my lips, it was as if shards of glass lodged in my throat. I buried myself in study, then in work, but deep within me a silence grew that time could never soften.

From afar, Da Chuan heard of her death and wrote to our mother: I am so sorry. She was too gentle, too pure for this world. I will remember her always.

Her husband performed grief like a play. At the funeral he bowed, spoke of her fragility, insisting "nothing could have been done." Within months he married the nurse who already carried his child.

At the close of the funeral, Ji Chang's cousin—a teacher—placed a worn notebook in my parents' hands. Ji Chang too had suffered: years in the countryside, illness, an early death. In that notebook he had guarded poems, many of them for Wen Wen—fragments of love and solitude that became, in her absence, the last echo of her voice.

Her journey had ended, but its thread was not cut.

CHAPTER 40

The Years That Followed

Time did not pause for grief.

A few years later, China began to change. Factories reopened, universities revived, doors once closed creaked open again. People spoke of reform and opening. High-rises rose from the old neighborhoods, shop windows filled with goods no one had seen before, and a new kind of hope quietly spread among the young.

But Wen Wen had not lived to see it.

Her son grew tall and handsome, carrying in his face a shadow of his mother's gentleness. He studied with quiet determination, was admitted to Fudan University, and in time became both a lecturer and a writer—living the dream that once belonged to her.

As for me, I followed another road. When the universities reopened, I seized the chance to study again. Later I was chosen to go abroad to America. There I built a new life, a family, and a career. Yet no matter how far I went, Wen Wen's absence traveled with me, a silence I could never escape.

Our parents grew old and passed away, laid to rest together as they had wished. After that, I stayed away for many years. I could not bring myself to return to the city of our youth, the city where her memory lingered in every street corner.

But time has a way of calling us back. When my hair turned white and my steps grew slower, I knew I had to return—to see once more the place where my parents and my sister now rested.

Epilogue · *The Day I Returned*

When I came back, the city was no longer the one we had known. Glass towers rose where alleys once lay. Neon spilled across the streets. Faces were open, unafraid children of a China my sister never lived to see.

I stopped at the university gates but could not bring myself to enter. Pride and sorrow lingered too heavily there. Instead, I walked to the cemetery.

Our parents rest together. A few steps away lies Wen Wen, alone. Her name is carved in stone, her years too few. I laid roses before her, my hands trembling with the words I had carried for decades.

"Jiejie," I whispered, "I am back. You should have seen this world—its changes, its hope. You should have seen your son: now a man, a teacher, a writer. You should have known love, peace, and time. None of us could give them to you."

The wind stirred; the pines whispered above me. I closed my eyes.

"I lived long," I said. "I crossed oceans, raised a family. But I never forgot you—not one day."

The city hummed in the distance, the present pressing forward. I knew I would not return again. But I had kept my promise: to stand beside her once more, to say she was not forgotten.

Her journey ended too soon. Mine draws toward its close. And yet, as I set the last rose upon her stone, I felt what endures—an unfinished thread carried forward by her son, by her memory, by the act of remembering.

The journey continues.

About the Author

Snow Ray is the pen name of a medical oncologist, physician-scientist and writer whose work bridges history, memory, and resilience. Through fiction, she gives voice to stories of love, silence, and survival, weaving intimate lives into the broader currents of history.